THE SMUGGLER

BY

ARTHUR B. REEVE

British Library Cataloguing-in-Publication Data
A catalogue record for this book is available from the
British Library

Arthur Benjamin Reeve

Arthur Benjamin Reeve was born on 15th October 1880 in New York, USA.

Reeve received his University education at Princeton and upon graduating enrolled at the New York Law School. However, his career was not destined to be in the field of Law. Between 1910 and 1918 he produced 82 short stories for Cosmopolitan magazine featuring his super-sleuth Professor Craig Kennedy. Kennedy is sometimes referred to as "The American Sherlock Holmes" due to his astounding ability at crime solving and his Watson-like sidekick Walter Jameson, a newspaper reporter. These characters featured in 18 novels, some of which were pseudo-novels stitched together from various short stories.

During this period he also began authoring screenplays, beginning with *The Exploits of Elaine* (1914). By the end of this decade his film career was at its peak with his name appearing on seven films, most of them serials and three of them starring Harry Houdini. Due to the film industry's migration to the west coast of America and Reeve's desire to remain in the east he produced less and less work for film. However, in 1927 he entered into a contract to write film scenarios for notorious millionaire-murderer, Harry K. Thaw, on the subject of fake spiritualists. The deal resulted in a lawsuit when Thaw refused to pay. In late 1928, Reeve declared bankruptcy.

Reeve continued to write detective stories for pulp magazines, but also covered many celebrated crime cases for various newspapers, including the murder of William Desmond Taylor, and the trial of Lindbergh baby kidnapper, Bruno Hauptmann. During the 1930s he became an anti-rackets crusader and produced a work of history on the subject titled *The Golden Age of Crime* (1931).

In 1932 he moved to Trenton to be near his alma mater. He died on 9th August 1936.

THE SMUGGLER

It was a rather sultry afternoon in the late summer when people who had calculated by the calendar rather than by the weather were returning to the city from the seashore, the mountains, and abroad.

Except for the week-ends, Kennedy and I had been pretty busy, though on this particular day there was a lull in the succession of cases which had demanded our urgent attention during the summer.

We had met at the Public Library, where Craig was doing some special research at odd moments in criminology. Fifth Avenue was still half deserted, though the few pedestrians who had returned or remained in town like ourselves were, as usual, to be found mostly on the west side of the street. Nearly everybody, I have noticed, walks on the one side of Fifth Avenue, winter or summer.

As we stood on the corner waiting for the traffic man's whistle to halt the crush of automobiles, a man on the top of a 'bus waved to Kennedy.

I looked up and caught a glimpse of Jack Herndon, an old college mate, who had had some political aspirations and had recently been appointed to a position in the customs house of New York. Herndon, I may add, represented the younger and clean-cut generation which is entering official life with great advantage to both themselves and politics.

The 'bus pulled up to the curb, and Jack tore down the breakneck steps hurriedly.

"I was just thinking of you, Craig," he beamed as we all shook hands, "and wondering whether you and Walter were in town. I think I should have come up to see you to-night, anyhow."

"Why, what's the matter - more, sugar frauds?" laughed Kennedy. "Or perhaps you have caught another art dealer red-handed?"

"No, not exactly," replied Herndon, growing graver for the moment. "We're having a big shake-up down at the office, none of your 'new broom' business, either. Real reform it is, this time."

"And you - are you going or coming?" inquired Craig with an interested twinkle.

"Coming, Craig, coming," answered Jack enthusiastically. "They've put me in charge of a sort of detective force as a special deputy surveyor to rout out some smuggling that we know is going on. If I make good it will go a long way for me - with all this talk of efficiency and economy down in Washington these days."

"What's on your mind now?" asked Kennedy observantly. "Can I help you in any way?" Herndon had taken each of us by an arm and walked us over to a stone bench in the shade of the library building.

"You have read the accounts in the afternoon papers of the peculiar death of Mademoiselle Violette, the little French modiste, up here on Forty-sixth Street?" he inquired.

"Yes," answered Kennedy. "What has that to do with customs reform?"

"A good deal, I fear," Herndon continued. "It's part of a case that has been bothering us all summer. It's the first really big thing I've been up against and it's as ticklish a bit of business as even a veteran treasury agent could wish."

Herndon looked thoughtfully at the passing crowd on the other side of the balustrade and continued. "It started, like many of our cases, with the anonymous letter writer. Early in the summer the letters began to come in to the deputy surveyor's office, all unsigned, though quite evidently written in a woman's hand, disguised of course, and on rather dainty notepaper. They warned us of a big plot to smuggle gowns and jewellery from Paris. Smuggling jewellery is pretty common because jewels take up little space and are very valuable. Perhaps it doesn't sound to you like a big thing to smuggle dresses, but when you realise that one of those filmy lacy creations may often be worth several hundred, if not thousand, dollars, and that it needs only a few of them on each ship that comes in to run up into the thousands, perhaps hundreds of thousands in a season, you will see how essential it is to break up that sort of thing. We've been getting after the individual private smugglers pretty sharply this summer and we've had lots of criticism. If we could land a big fellow and make an object-lesson of the extent of the thing I believe it would leave our critics of the press without a leg to stand on.

"At least that was why I was interested in the letters. But it was not until a few days ago that we got a tip that gave us a real working clue, for the anonymous letters had been very vague as to names, dates, and places, though bold enough as to general charges, as if the writer were fearful of incriminating herself - or himself. Strange to say, this new clue came from the wife of one of the customs men. She happened to be in a Broadway manicure shop one day when she heard a woman talking with the manicurist about fall styles, and she was all attention when she heard the customer say, 'You remember Mademoiselle Violette's - that place that had the exquisite things straight from Paris, and so cheaply, too? Well, Violette says she'll have to raise her prices so that they will be nearly as high as the regular stores. She says the tariff has gone up, or something, but it hasn't, has it?"

"The manicurist laughed knowingly, and the next remark caught the woman's attention. 'No, indeed. But then, I guess she meant that she had to pay the duty now. You know they are getting much stricter. To tell the truth, I imagine most of Violette's goods were - well - '

"'Smuggled?' supplied the customer in an undertone.

"The manicurist gave a slight shrug of the shoulders and a bright little yes of a laugh.

"That was all. But it was enough. I set a special customs officer to watch Mademoiselle, a clever fellow. He didn't have time to find out much, but on the other hand I am sure he didn't do anything to alarm Mademoiselle. That would have been a bad game. His case was progressing favourably and he had become acquainted with one of the girls who worked in the shop. We might have got some evidence, but suddenly this morning he walked up to my desk and handed me an early edition of an afternoon paper. Mademoiselle Violette had been discovered dead in her shop by the girls when they came to work this morning. Apparently she had been there all night, but the report was quite indefinite and I am on my way up there now to meet the coroner, who has agreed to wait for me."

"You think there is some connection between her death and the letters?" put in Craig.

"Of course I can't say, yet," answered Herndon dubiously. "The papers seem to think it was a suicide. But then why should she commit suicide? My man found out that among the girls it was common gossip that she was to marry Jean Pierre, the Fifth Avenue jeweller, of the firm of Lang & Pierre down on the next block. Pierre is due in New York on La Montaigne to-night or to-morrow morning.

"Why, if my suspicions are correct, it is this Pierre who is the brains of the whole affair. And here's another thing. You know we have a sort of secret service in Paris and other European cities which is constantly keeping an eye on purchases of goods by Americans abroad. Well, the chief of our men in Paris cables me that Pierre is known to have made extraordinarily heavy purchases of made-up jewellery this season. For one thing, we believe he has acquired from a syndicate a rather famous diamond necklace which it has taken years to assemble and match up, worth about three hundred thousand. You know the duty on made-up jewellery is sixty per cent., and even if he brought the stones in loose it would be ten per cent., which on a valuation of, say, two hundred thousand, means twenty thousand dollars duty alone. Then he has a splendid 'dog collar' of pearls, and, oh, a lot of other stuff. I know because we get our tips from all sorts of sources and they are usually pretty straight. Some come from dealers who are sore about not making sales themselves. So you see there is a good deal at stake in this case and it may be that in following it out we shall kill more than one bird. I wish you'd come along with me up to Mademoiselle Violette's and give me an opinion."

Craig had already risen from the bench and we were walking up the Avenue.

The establishment of Mademoiselle Violette consisted of a three-story and basement brownstone house in which the basement and first floor had been remodelled for business purposes. Mademoiselle's place, which was on the first floor, was announced to the world by a neat little oval gilt sign on the hand railing of the steps.

We ascended and rang the bell. As we waited I noticed that there were several other modistes on the same street, while almost directly across was a sign which proclaimed that on September 15 Mademoiselle Gabrielle would open with a high class exhibition of imported gowns from Paris.

We entered. The coroner and an undertaker were already there, and the former was expecting Herndon. Kennedy and I had already met him and he shook hands cordially.

Mademoiselle Violette, it seemed, had rented the entire house and then had sublet the basement to a milliner, using the first floor herself, the second as a workroom for the girls whom she employed, while she lived on the top floor, which had been fitted for light housekeeping with a kitchenette. It was in the back room of the shop itself on the first floor that her body had been discovered, lying on a davenport.

"The newspaper reports were very indefinite," began Herndon, endeavouring to take in the situation. "I suppose they told nearly all the story, but what caused her death? Have you found that out yet? Was it poison or violence?

The coroner said nothing, but with a significant glance at Kennedy he drew a peculiar contrivance from his pocket. It had four round holes in it and through each hole he slipped a finger, then closed his hand, and exhibited his clenched fist. It looked as if he wore a series of four metal rings on his fingers.

"Brass knuckles?" suggested Herndon, looking hastily at the body, which showed not a sign of violence on the stony face.

The coroner shook his head knowingly. Suddenly he raised his fist. I saw him press hard with his thumb on the upper end of the metal contrivance. From the other end, just concealed under his little linger, there shot out as if released by a magic spring a thin keen little blade of the brightest and toughest steel. He was holding, instead of a meaningless contrivance of four rings, a most dangerous kind of stiletto or dagger upraised. He lifted his thumb and the blade sprang back into its sheath like an extinguished spark of light.

"An Apache dagger, such as is used in the underworld of Paris," broke out Kennedy, his eyes gleaming with interest.

The coroner nodded. "We found it," he said, "clasped loosely in her hand. But it is only by expert medical testimony that we can determine whether it was placed on her fingers before or after this happened. We have photographed it, and the prints are being developed."

He had now uncovered the slight figure of the little French modiste. On the dress, instead of the profuse flow of blood which we had expected to see, there was a single round spot. And in the white marble skin of her breast was a little, nearly microscopic puncture, directly over the heart.

"She must have died almost instantly," commented Kennedy, glancing from the Apache weapon to the dead woman and back again. "Internal hemorrhage. I suppose you have searched her effects. Have you found anything that gives a hint among them?"

"No," replied the coroner doubtfully, "I can't say we have - unless it is the bundle of letters from Pierre, the jeweller. They seem to have been engaged, and yet the letters stopped abruptly, and, well, from the tone of the last one from him I should say there was a quarrel brewing."

An exclamation from Herndon followed. "The same notepaper and the same handwriting as the anonymous letters," he cried.

But that was all. Go over the ground as Kennedy might he could find nothing further than the coroner and Herndon had already revealed.

"About these people, Lang & Pierre," asked Craig thoughtfully when we had left Mademoiselle's and were riding downtown to the customs house with Herndon. "What do you know about them? I presume that Lang is in America, if his partner is abroad."

"Yes, he is here in New York. I believe the firm has a rather unsavoury reputation; they have to be watched, I am told. Then, too, one or the other of the partners makes frequent trips abroad, mostly Pierre. Pierre, as you see, was very intimate with Mademoiselle, and the letters simply confirm what the girls told my detective. He was believed to be engaged to her and I see no reason now to doubt that. The fact is, Kennedy, it wouldn't surprise me in the least to learn that it was he who engineered the smuggling for her as well as himself."

"What about the partner? What role does he play in your suspicions?"

"That's another curious feature. Lang doesn't seem to bother much with the business. He is a sort of silent partner, although nominally the head of the firm. Still, they both seem always to be plentifully supplied with money and to have a good trade. Lang lives most of the time up on the west shore of the Hudson, and seems to be more interested in his position as commodore of the Riverledge Yacht Club than in his business down here. He is quite a sport, a great motor-boat enthusiast, and has lately taken to hydroplanes."

"I meant," repeated Kennedy, "what about Lang and Mademoiselle Violette. Were they - ah - friendly?"

"Oh," replied Herndon, seeming to catch the idea. "I see. Of course - Pierre abroad and Lang here. I see what you mean. Why, the girl told my man that Mademoiselle Violette used to go motor-boating with Lang, but only when her fiance, Pierre, was along. No, I don't think she ever had anything to do with Lang, if that's what you are driving at.

He may have paid attentions to her, but Pierre was her lover, and I haven't a doubt but that if Lang made any advances she repelled them. She seems to have thought everything of Pierre."

We had reached Herndon's office by this time. Leaving word with his stenographer to get the very latest reports from La Montaigne, he continued talking to us about his work.

Dressmakers, milliners, and jewellers are our worst offenders now," he remarked as we stood gazing out of the window at the panorama of the bay off the sea-wall of the Battery. "Why, time and again we unearth what looks for all the world like a 'dressmakers' syndicate,' though this case is the first I've had that involved a death. Really, I've come to look on smuggling as one of the fine arts among crimes. Once the smuggler, like the pirate and the highwayman, was a sort of gentleman-rogue. But now it has become a very ladylike art. The extent of it is almost beyond belief, too. It begins with the steerage and runs right up to the absolute unblushing cynicism of the first cabin. I suppose you know that women, particularly a certain brand of society women, are the worst and most persistent offenders. Why, they even boast of it. Smuggling isn't merely popular, it's aristocratic. But we're going to take some of the flavour out of it before we finish."

He tore open a cable message which a boy had brought in. "Now, take this, for instance," he continued. "You remember the sign across the street from Mademoiselle Violette's, announcing that a Mademoiselle Gabrielle was going to open a salon or whatever they call it? Well, here's another cable from our Paris Secret Service with a belated tip. They tell us to look out for a Mademoiselle Gabrielle on La Montaigne, too. That's another interesting thing. You know the various lines are all ranked, at least in our estimation, according to the likelihood of such offences being perpetrated by their passengers. We watch ships from London, Liverpool, and Paris most carefully. Scandinavian ships are the least likely to need watching. Well, Miss Roberts?"

"We have just had a wireless about La Montaigne," reported his stenographer, who had entered while he was speaking, " and she is three hundred miles east of Sandy Hook. She won't dock until tomorrow."

"Thank you. Well, fellows, it is getting late and that means nothing more doing to-night. Can you be here early in the morning? We'll go down the bay and 'bring in the ship,' as our men call it when the deputy surveyor and his acting deputies go down to meet it at Quarantine. I can't tell you how much I appreciate your kindness in helping me. If my men get anything connecting Lang with Mademoiselle Violette's case I'll let you know immediately."

It was a bright clear snappy morning, in contrast with the heat of the day before, when we boarded the revenue tug at the Barge Office. The waters of the harbour never looked more blue as they danced in the early sunlight, flecked here and there by a foaming whitecap as the conflicting tides eddied about. The shores of Staten Island were almost as green as in the spring, and even the haze over the Brooklyn factories had lifted. It looked almost like a stage scene, clear and sharp, new and brightly coloured.

Perhaps the least known and certainly one of the least recognised of the government services is that which includes the vigilant ships of the revenue service. It was not a revenue cutter, however, on which we were ploughing down the bay. The cutter lay, white and gleaming in the morning sun, at anchor off Stapleton, like a miniature warship, saluting as we passed. The revenue boats which steam down to Quarantine and make fast to the incoming ocean greyhounds are revenue tugs.

Down the bay we puffed and buffeted for about forty minutes before we arrived at the little speck of an island that is Quarantine. Long before we were there we sighted the great La Montaigne near the group of buildings on the island, where she had been waiting since early morning for the tide and the customs officials. The tug steamed alongside, and quickly up the high ladders swarmed the boarding officer and the deputy collectors. We followed Herndon straight to the main saloon, where the collectors began to receive the declarations which had been made out on blanks furnished to the passengers on the voyage over. They had had several days to write them out - the less excuse for omissions.

Glancing at each hastily the collector detached from it the slip with the number at the bottom and handed the number back, to be presented at the inspector's desk at the pier, where customs inspectors were assigned in turn.

"Number 140 is the one we want to watch," I heard Herndon whisper to Kennedy. "That tall dark fellow over there."

I followed his direction cautiously and saw a sparely built, striking looking man who had just filed his declaration and was chatting vivaciously with a lady who was just about to file hers. She was a clinging looking little thing with that sort of doll-like innocence that deceives nobody.

"No, you don't have to swear to it," he said. "You used to do that, but now you simply sign your name and take a chance," he added, smiling and showing a row of perfect teeth.

"Number 156," Herndon noted as the collector detached the stub and handed it to her. "That was Mademoiselle Gabrielle."

The couple passed out to the deck, still chatting gaily.

"In the old days, before they got to be so beastly particular," I heard him say, "I always used to get the courtesy of the port, an official expedite. But that is over now."

The ship was now under way, her flags snapping in the brisk coolish breeze that told of approaching autumn. We had passed up the lower bay and the Narrows, and the passengers were crowded forward to catch the first glimpse of the skyscrapers of New York.

On up the bay we ploughed, throwing the spray proudly as we went. Herndon employed the time in keeping a sharp watch on the tall, thin man. Incidentally he sought out the wireless operator and from him learned that a code wireless message had been received for Pierre, apparently from his partner, Lang.

"There is no mention of anything dutiable in this declaration by 140 which corresponds with any of the goods mentioned in the first cable from Paris," a collector remarked unobtrusively to Herndon, "nor in 156 corresponding to the second cable."

"I didn't suppose there would be," was his laconic reply. "That's our job - to find the stuff."

At last La Montaigne was warped into the dock. The piles of first-class baggage on the ship were raucously deposited on the wharf and slowly the passengers filed down the plank to meet the line of white-capped uniformed inspectors and plain-clothes appraisers. The comedy and tragedy of the customs inspection had begun.

We were among the first to land. Herndon took up a position from which he could see without being seen. In the semi-light of the little windows in the enclosed sides of the pier, under the steel girders of the arched roof like a vast hall, there was a panorama of a huge mass of open luggage.

At last Number 140 came down, alone, to the roped-off dock. He walked nonchalantly over to the little deputy surveyor's desk, and an inspector was quickly assigned to him. It was all done neatly in the regular course of business apparently. He did not know that in the orderly rush the sharpest of Herndon's men had been picked out, much as a trick card player will force a card on his victim.

Already the customs inspection was well along. One inspector had been assigned to about each five passengers, and big piles of finery were being remorselessly tumbled out in shapeless heaps and exposed to the gaze of that part of the public which was not too much concerned over the same thing as to its own goods and chattels. Reticules and purses were being inspected. Every trunk was presumed to have a false bottom, and things wrapped up in paper were viewed suspiciously and unrolled. Clothes were being shaken and pawed. There did not seem to be much opportunity for concealment.

Herndon now had donned the regulation straw hat of the appraiser, and accompanied by us, posing as visitors, was sauntering about. At last we came within earshot of the spot where the inspector was going through the effects of 140.

Out of the corner of my eyes I could see that a dispute was in progress over some trifling matter. The man was cool and calm. "Call the appraiser, he said at last, with the air of a man standing on his rights. "I object to this frisking of passengers. Uncle Sam is little better than a pickpocket. Besides, I cans I wait here all day. My partner is waiting for me uptown."

Herndon immediately took notice. But it was quite evidently, after all, only an altercation for the benefit of those who were watching. I am sure he knew he was being watched, but as the dispute proceeded he assumed the look of a man keenly amused. The matter, involving only a few dollars, was finally adjusted by his yielding gracefully and with an air of resignation. Still Herndon did not go and I am sure it annoyed him.

Suddenly he turned and faced Herndon. I could not help thinking, in spite of all that he must be so expert, that, if he really were a smuggler, he had all the poise and skill at evasion that would entitle him to be called a past master of the art.

"You see that woman over there? "he whispered. "She says she is just coming home after studying music in Paris."

We looked. It was the guileless ingenue, Mademoiselle Gabrielle.

"She has dutiable goods, all right. I saw her declaration. She is trying to bring in as personal effects of a foreign resident gowns which, I believe, she intends to wear on the stage. She's an actress."

There was nothing for Herndon to do but to act on the tip. The man had got rid of us temporarily, but we knew the inspector would be, if anything, more vigilant. I think he took even longer than usual.

Mademoiselle Gabrielle and her maid pouted and fussed over the renewed examination which Herndon ordered. According to the inspector everything was new and expensive; according to her, old, shabby, and cheap. She denied everything, raged and threatened. But when, instead of ordering the stamp "Passed" to be placed on her half dozen trunks and bags which contained in reality only a few dutiable articles, Herndon threatened to order them to the appraiser's stores and herself to go to the Law Division if she did not admit the points in dispute, there was a real scene.

"Generally, madame," he remonstrated, though I could see he was baffled at finding nothing of the goods he had really expected to find, "generally even for a first offence the goods are confiscated and the court or district attorney is content to let the person off with a fine. If this happens again we'll be more severe. So you had better pay the duty on these few little matters, without that."

If he had been expecting to "throw a scare "into her, it did not succeed. "Well, I suppose if I must, I must," she said, and the only result of the diversion was that she paid a few dollars more than had been expected and went off in a high state of mind.

Herndon had disappeared for a moment, after a whisper from Kennedy, to instruct two of his men to shadow Mademoiselle Gabrielle and, later, Pierre. He soon rejoined us and we casually returned to the vicinity of our tall friend, Number 140, for whom I felt even less respect than ever after his apparently ungallant action toward the lady he had been talking with. He seemed to notice my attitude and he remarked defensively for my benefit, "Only a patriotic act."

His inspector by this time had finished a most minute examination. There was nothing that could be discovered, not a false book with a secret spring that might disclose instead of reading matter a heap of almost priceless jewels, not a suspicious bulging of any garment or of the lining of a trunk or grip. Some of the goods might have been on his person, but not much, and certainly there was no excuse for ordering a personal examination, for he could not have hidden a tenth part of what we knew he had, even under the proverbial porous plaster. He was impeccable. Accordingly there was nothing for the inspector to do but to declare a polite armistice.

"So you didn't find 'Mona Lisa' in a false bottom, and my trunks were not lined with smuggled cigars after all," he rasped savagely as the stamp "Passed" was at last affixed and he paid in cash at the little window with its sign, "Pay Duty

Here: U.S. Custom House," some hundred dollars instead of the thousands Herndon had been hoping to collect, if not to seize.

All through the inspection, an extra close scrutiny had been kept on the other passengers as well, to prevent any of them from being in league with the smugglers, though there was no direct or indirect evidence to show that any of the others were.

We were about to leave the wharf, also, when Craig's attention was called to a stack of trunks still remaining.

"Whose are those?" he asked as he lifted one. It felt suspiciously light.

"Some of them belong to a Mr. Pierre and the rest to a Miss Gabrielle," answered an inspector. "Bonded for Troy and waiting to be transferred by the express company."

Here, perhaps, at last was an explanation, and Craig took advantage of it. Could it be that the real seat of trouble was not here but at some other place, that some exchange was to be made en route or perhaps an attempt at bribery?

Herndon, too, was willing to run a risk. He ordered the trunks opened immediately. But to our disappointment they were almost empty. There was scarcely a thing of value in them. Most of the contents consisted of clothes that had plainly been made in America and were being brought back here. It was another false scent. We had been played with and baffled at every turn. Perhaps this had been the method originally agreed on. At any rate it had been changed.

"Could they have left the goods in Paris, after all?" I queried.

"With the fall and winter trade just coming on?" Kennedy replied, with an air of finality that set at rest any doubts about his opinion on that score. "I thought perhaps we had a case of what do you call it, Herndon, when they leave trunks that are to be secretly removed by dishonest expressmen from the wharf at night?

"Sleepers. Oh, we've broken that up, too. No expressman would dare try it now. I must confess this thing is beyond me, Craig."

Kennedy made no answer. Evidently there was nothing to do but to await developments and see what Herndon's men reported. We had been beaten at every turn in the game. Herndon seemed to feel that there was a bitter sting in the defeat, particularly because the smuggler or smugglers had actually been in our grasp so long to do with as we pleased, and had so cleverly slipped out again, leaving us holding the bag.

Kennedy was especially thoughtful as he told over the facts of the case in his mind. "Of course," he remarked, " Mademoiselle Gabrielle wasn't an actress. But we can't deny that she had very little that would justify Herndon in holding her, unless he simply wants a newspaper row."

"But I thought Pierre was quite intimate with her at first," I ventured. "That was a dirty trick of his."

Craig laughed. "You mean an old one. That was simply a blind, to divert attention from himself. I suspect they talked that over between themselves for days before."

It was plainly more perplexing than ever. What had happened? Had Pierre been a prestidigitator and had he merely said presto when our backs were turned and whisked the goods invisibly into the country? I could find no explanation for the little drama on the pier. If Herndon's men had any genius in detecting smuggling, their professional opponent certainly had greater genius in perpetrating it.

We did not see Herndon again until after a hasty luncheon. He was in his office and inclined to take a pessimistic view of the whole affair. He brightened up when a telephone message came in from one of his shadows. The men trailing Pierre and Mademoiselle Gabrielle had crossed trails and run together at a little French restaurant on the lower West Side, where Pierre, Lang, and Mademoiselle Gabrielle had met and were dining in a most friendly spirit. Kennedy was right. She had been merely a cog in the machinery of the plot.

The man reported that even when a newsboy had been sent in by him with the afternoon papers displaying in big headlines the mystery of the death of Mademoiselle Violette, they had paid no attention. It seemed evident that whatever the fate of the little modiste, Mademoiselle Gabrielle had quite replaced her in the affections of Pierre. There was nothing for us to do but to separate and await developments.

It was late in the afternoon when Craig and I received a hurried message from Herndon. One of his men had just called him up over long distance from Riverledge. The party had left the restaurant hurriedly, and though they had taken the only taxicab in sight he had been able to follow them in time to find out that they were going up to Riverledge. They were now preparing to go out for a sail in one of Lang's motor-boats and he would be unable, of course, to follow them further.

For the remainder of the afternoon Kennedy remained pondering the case. At last an idea seemed to dawn on him. He found Herndon still at his office and made an appointment to meet on the waterfront near La Montaigne's pier, after dinner. The change in Kennedy's spirits was obvious, though it did not in the least enlighten my curiosity. Even after a dinner which was lengthened out considerably, I thought, I did not get appreciably nearer a solution, for we strolled over to the laboratory, where Craig loaded me down with a huge package which was wrapped up in heavy paper.

We arrived on the corner opposite the wharf just as it was growing dusk. The neighbourhood did not appeal to me at night, and even though there were two of us I was rather glad when we met Herndon, who was waiting in the shadow of a fruit stall.

But instead of proceeding across to the pier by the side of which La Montaigne was moored, we cut across the wide street and turned down the next pier, where a couple of freighters were lying. The odour of salt water, sewage, rotting wood, and the night air was not inspiring. Nevertheless I was now carried away with the strangeness of our adventure.

Halfway down the pier Kennedy paused before one of the gangways that was shrouded in darkness. The door was opened and we followed gingerly across the dirty deck of the freight ship. Below we could hear the water lapping the piles of the pier. Across a dark abyss lay the grim monster La Montaigne with here and there a light gleaming on one of her decks. The sounds of the city seemed miles away.

"What a fine place for a murder," laughed Kennedy coolly. He was unwrapping the package which he had taken from me. It proved to be a huge reflector in front of which was placed a little arrangement which, under the light of a shaded lantern carried by Herndon, looked like a coil of wire of some kind.

To the back of the reflector Craig attached two other flexible wires which led to a couple of dry cells and a cylinder with a broadened end, made of vulcanised rubber. It might have been a telephone receiver, for all I could tell in the darkness.

While I was still speculating on the possible use of the enormous parabolic reflector, a slight commotion on the opposite side of the pier distracted my attention. A ship was coming in and was being carefully and quietly berthed alongside the other big iron freighter on that side. Herndon had left us.

"The Mohican is here," he remarked as he rejoined us. To my look of inquiry he added, "The revenue cutter."

Kennedy had now finished and had pointed the reflector full at La Montaigne. With a whispered hasty word of caution and advice to Herndon, he drew me along with him down the wharf again.

At the little door which was cut in the barrier guarding the shore end of La Montaigne's wharf Kennedy stopped. The customs service night watchman - there is always a watchman of some kind aboard every ship, passenger or freighter, all the time she is in port - seemed to understand, for he admitted us after a word with Kennedy.

Threading our way carefully among the boxes, and bales, and crates which were piled high, we proceeded down the wharf. Under the electric lights the longshoremen were working feverishly, for the unloading and loading of a giant transAtlantic vessel in the rush season is a long and tedious process at best, requiring night work and overtime, for every moment, like every cubic foot of space, counts.

Once within the door, however, no one paid much attention to us. They seemed to take it for granted that we had some right there. We boarded the ship by one of the many entrances and then proceeded down to a deck where apparently no one was working. It was more like a great house than a ship, I felt, and I wondered whether Kennedy's search was not more of a hunt for a needle in a haystack than anything else. Yet he seemed to know what he was after.

We had descended to what I imagined must be the quarters of the steward. About us were many large cases and chests, stacked up and marked as belonging to the ship. Kennedy's attention was attracted to them immediately. All at once it flashed on me what his purpose was. In some of those cases were the smuggled goods!

Before I could say a word and before Kennedy had a chance even to try to verify his suspicions, a sudden approach of footsteps startled us. He drew me into a cabin or room full of shelves with ship's stores.

"Why didn't you bring Herndon over and break into the boxes, if you think the stuff is hidden in one of them?" I whispered.

"And let those higher up escape while their tools take all the blame?" he answered. "Sh-h."

The men who had come into the compartment looked about as if expecting to see some one.

"Two of them came down," a gruff voice said. "Where are they?"

>From the noise I inferred that there must be four or five men, and from the ease with which they shifted the cases about some of them must have been pretty husky stevedores.

"I don't know," a more polished but unfamiliar voice answered.

The door to our hiding-place was opened roughly and then banged shut before we realised it. With a taunting laugh, some one turned a key in the lock and before we could move a quick shift of packing cases against the door made escape impossible.

Here we were marooned, shanghaied, as it were, within sight if not call of Herndon and our friends. We had run up against professional smugglers, of whom I had vaguely read, disguised as stewards, deckhands, stokers, and other workers.

The only other opening to the cabin was a sort of porthole, more for ventilation than anything else. Kennedy stuck his head through it, but it was impossible for a man to squeeze out. There was one of the lower decks directly before us while a bright arc light gleamed tantalisingly over it, throwing a round circle of light into our prison. I reflected bitterly on our shipwreck within sight of port.

Kennedy remained silent, and I did not know what was working in his mind. Together we made out the outline of the freighter at the next wharf and speculated as to the location where we had left Herndon with the huge reflector. There was no moon and it was as black as ink in that direction, but if we could have got out I would have trusted to luck to reach it by swimming.

Below us, from the restless water lapping on the sides of the hulk of La Montaigne, we could now hear muffled sounds. It was a motor-boat which had come crawling up the river front, with lights extinguished, and had pushed a cautious nose into the slip where our ship lay at the quay. None of your romantic low-lying, rakish craft of the old smuggling yarns was this, ready for deeds of desperation in the dark hours of midnight. It was just a modern little motor-boat, up-to-date, and swift.

"Perhaps we'll get out of this finally," I grumbled as I understood now what was afoot, "but not in time to be of any use."

A smothered sound as of something going over the vessel's side followed. It was one of the boxes which we had seen outside in the storeroom. Another followed, and a third and a fourth.

Then came a subdued parley. "We have two customs detectives locked in a cabin here. We can't stay now. You'll have to take us and our things off, too."

"Can't do it," called up another muffled voice. "Make your things into a little bundle. We'll take that, but you'll have to get past the night-watchman yourselves and meet us at Riverledge."

A moment later something else went over the side, and from the sound we could infer that the engine of the motor-boat was being started.

A Voice sounded mockingly outside our door. "Bon soir, you fellows in there. We're going up the dock. Sorry to leave you here till morning, but they'll let you out then. Au revoir."

Below I could hear just the faintest well-muffled chug-chug. Kennedy in the meantime had been coolly craning his neck out of our porthole under the rays of the arc light overhead. He was holding something in his hand. It seemed like a little silver-backed piece of thin glass with a flaring funnel-like thing back of it, which he held most particularly. Though he heard the parting taunt outside he paid no attention.

"You go to the deuce, whoever you are," I cried, beating on the door, to which only a coarse laugh echoed back down the passageway.

"Be quiet, Walter," ordered Kennedy. "We have located the smuggled goods in the storeroom of the steward, four wooden cases of them. I think the stuff must have been brought on the ship in the trunks and then transferred to the cases, perhaps after the code wireless message was received. But we have been overpowered and locked in a cabin with a port too small to crawl through. The cases have been lowered over the side of the ship to a motor-boat that was waiting below. The lights on the boat are out, but if you hurry you can get it. The accomplices who locked us in are going to disappear up the wharf. If you could only get the night watchman quickly enough you could catch them, too, before they reach the street."

I had turned, half expecting to see Kennedy talking to a ship's officer who might have chanced on the deck outside. There was no one. The only thing of life was the still sputtering arc light. Had the man gone crazy?

"What of it?" I growled. "Don't you suppose I know all that? What's the use of repeating it now? The thing to do is to get out of this hole. Come, help me at this door. Maybe we can batter it down."

Kennedy paid no attention to me, however, but kept his eyes glued on the Cimmerian blackness outside the porthole.

He had done nothing apparently, yet a long finger of light seemed to shoot out into the sky from the pier across from us and begin waving back and forth as it was lowered to the dark waters of the river. It was a searchlight. At once I thought of the huge reflector which I had seen set up. But that had been on our side of the next pier and this light came from the far side where the Mohican lay.

"What is it?" I asked eagerly. "What has happened?"

It was as if a prayer had been answered from our dungeon on La Montaigne.

"I knew we should need some means to communicate with Herndon," he explained simply, "and the wireless telephone wasn't practicable. So I have used Dr. Alexander Graham Bell's photophone. Any of the lights on this side of La Montaigne, I knew, would serve. What I did, Walter, was merely to talk into the mouthpiece back of this little silvered mirror which reflects light. The vibrations of the voice caused a diaphragm in it to vibrate and thus the beam of reflected light was made to pulsate. In other words, this little thing is just a simple apparatus to transform the air vibrations of the voice into light vibrations.

"The parabolic reflector over there catches these light vibrations and focuses them on the cell of selenium which you perhaps noticed in the centre of the reflector. You remember doubtless that the element selenium varies its electrical resistance under light? Thus there are reproduced similar variations in the cell to those vibrations here in this transmitter. The cell is connected with a telephone receiver and batteries over there and there you are. It is very simple. In the ordinary carbon telephone transmitter a variable electrical resistance is produced by pressure, since carbon is not so good a conductor under pressure. Then these variations are transmitted along two wires. This photophone is wireless. Selenium even emits notes under a vibratory beam of light, the pitch depending on the frequency. Changes in the intensity of the light focused by the reflector on the cell alter its electrical resistance and vary the current from the dry batteries. Hence the telephone receiver over there is affected. Bell used the photophone or radiophone over several hundred feet, Ruhmer over several miles. When you thought I was talking to myself I was really telling Herndon what had happened and what to do - talking to him literally over a beam of light."

I could scarcely believe it, but an exclamation from Kennedy as he drew his head in quickly recalled my attention. "Look out on the river, Walter," he cried. "The Mohican has her searchlight sweeping up and down. What do you see?"

The long finger of light had now come to rest. In its pathway I saw a lightless motor-boat bobbing up and down, crowding on all speed, yet followed relentlessly by the accusing finger. The river front was now alive with shouting.

Suddenly the Mohican shot out from behind the pier where she had been hidden. In spite of Lang's expertness it was an unequal race. Nor would it have made much difference if it had been otherwise, for a shot rang out from the Mohican which commanded instant respect. The powerful revenue cutter rapidly overhauled the little craft.

A hurried tread down the passageway followed. Cases were being shoved aside and a key in the door of our compartment turned quickly. I waited with clenched fists, prepared for an attack.

"You're all right?" Herndon's voice inquired anxiously. "We've got that steward and the other fellows all right."

"Yes, come on," shouted Craig. "The cutter has made a capture."

We had reached the stern of the ship, and far out in the river the Mohican was now headed toward us. She came alongside, and Herndon quickly seized a rope, fastened it to the rail, and let himself down to the deck of the cutter. Kennedy and I followed.

"This is a high-handed proceeding," I heard a voice that must have been Lang's protesting. "By what right do you stop me? You shall suffer for this."

"The Mohican," broke in Herndon, "has the right to appear anywhere from Southshoal Lightship off Nantucket to the capes of the Delaware, demand an inspection of any vessel's manifest and papers, board anything from La Montaigne to your little motor-boat, inspect it, seize it, if necessary put a crew on it." He slapped the little cannon. "That commands respect. Besides, you were violating the regulations - no lights."

On the deck of the cutter now lay four cases. A man broke one of them open, then another. Inside he disclosed thousands of dollars' worth of finery, while from a tray he drew several large chamois bags of glittering diamonds and pearls.

Pierre looked on, crushed, all his jauntiness gone.

"So," exclaimed Kennedy, facing him, "you have your jilted fiancee, Mademoiselle Violette, to thank for this - her letters and her suicide. It wasn't as easy as you thought to throw her over for a new soul mate, this Mademoiselle Gabrielle whom you were going to set up as a rival in business to Violette. Violette has her revenge for making a plaything of her heart, and if the dead can take any satisfaction she"

With a quick movement Kennedy anticipated a motion of Pierre's. The ruined smuggler had contemplated either an attack on himself or his captor, but Craig had seized him by the wrist and ground his knuckles into the back of Pierre's clenched fist until he winced with pain. An Apache dagger similar to that which the little modiste had used to end her life tragedy clattered to the deck of the ship, a mute testimonial to the high class of society Pierre and his associates must have cultivated.

"None of that, Pierre," Craig muttered, releasing him. "You can't cheat the government out of its just dues even in the matter of punishment."